DOGS
don't do *Ballet*

For Amber, James, Lauren and Isaac, with love – AK

For Michael (believer in Biff) – SO

SIMON AND SCHUSTER
First published in Great Britain in 2010 by Simon and Schuster UK Ltd
1st Floor, 222 Gray's Inn Road, London WC1X 8HB
A CBS Company

Text copyright © 2010 Anna Kemp
Illustrations copyright © 2010 Sara Ogilvie

The right of Anna Kemp and Sara Ogilvie to be identified as
the author and illustrator of this work has been asserted by them
in accordance with the Copyright, Designs and Patents Act, 1988

A CIP catalogue record for this book is available from the British Library upon request

ISBN: 978-1-84738-473-7 (HB)
ISBN: 978-1-84738-474-4 (PB)

Printed in China
1 3 5 7 9 10 8 6 4 2

DOGS
don't do Ballet

Anna Kemp

Illustrated by Sara Ogilvie

SIMON AND SCHUSTER

London   New York   Sydney

My dog is not like other dogs.

He doesn't do dog stuff like weeing on lampposts,
or scratching his fleas, or drinking out of the toilet.

If I throw him a stick,

he looks at me like I'm crazy.

So I have to fetch it myself.

No, my dog likes music and moonlight and walking on his tiptoes.

You see, my dog doesn't think he's a dog . . .

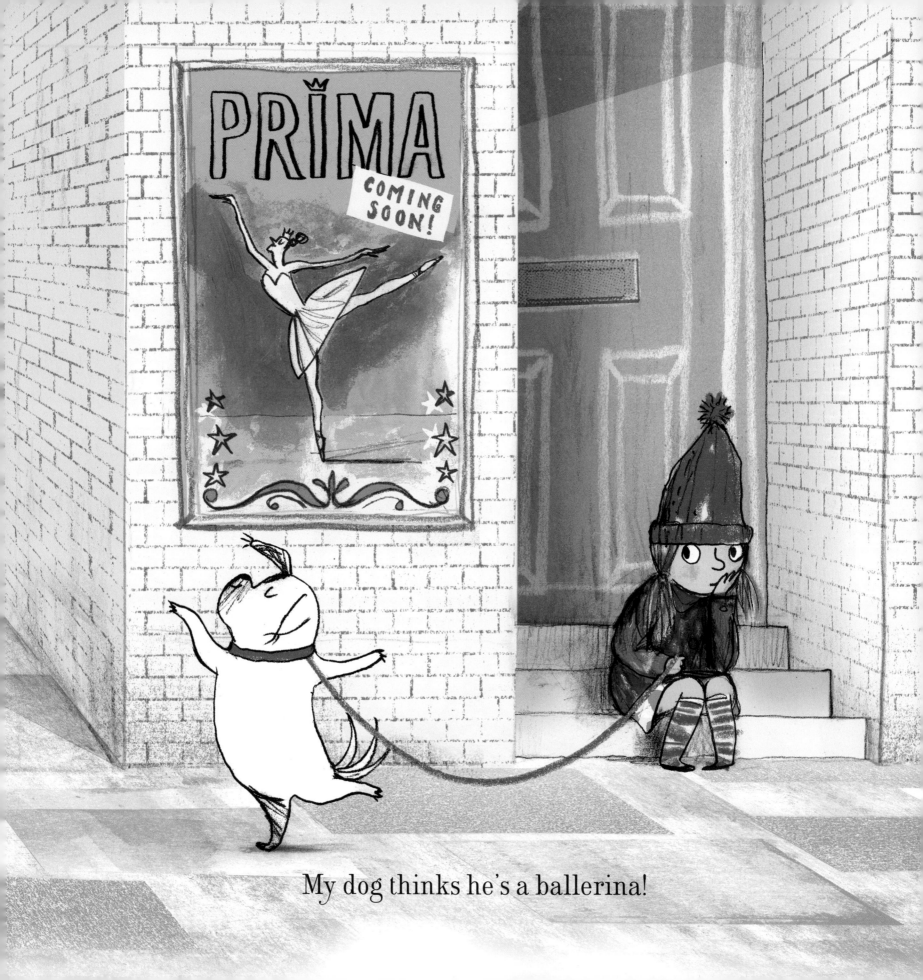

My dog thinks he's a ballerina!

When I get ready for ballet class, he looks longingly at my tutu and ballet shoes and I just know he is dreaming of his name in lights.

"Dad," I say. "Can Biff come too? He loves ballet."
"Not a chance," says Dad. "Dogs don't do ballet!"

Then, one Saturday on my way to class, I get a funny
feeling. A funny feeling that I am being watched.
A funny feeling that I am being followed.

When Miss Polly is teaching us a new routine, I think I see something peeking in at the window. Something with a wet nose. Something with a tail.

"Right girls," says Miss Polly. "Who's going to demonstrate first position?"

But, before anyone can step forward, there is a loud bark from the back of the hall and something furry rushes to the front.

"What is this?" asks Miss Polly, peering over her glasses.

"This," I say, "is my dog."

"Well take it away at once," says Miss Polly,
wrinkling up her nose. "Dogs don't do ballet!"
My poor dog stops wagging his tail and
his ears droop down at the ends.

I take my dog home and give him a bowl of
Doggie-Donuts. But he won't touch them.

He just stays in his kennel for days and
days, and at night he howls at the moon.

For my birthday I get tickets for the Royal Ballet.
"Can Biff come too?" I ask Dad. "He loves ballet."
My dog pricks up his ears and wags his tail.

"No," says Dad. "If I've told you once,
I've told you a thousand times: dogs don't do ballet!"

As we wait for the bus I think about my
poor old dog, all on his own, howling at the moon.
Then I get a funny feeling.

A funny feeling that I am being watched.

A funny feeling that I am not alone.

The ballet is magical!
The orchestra plays as the prima ballerina dances
and prances, and twirls and whirls, and skips and . . .

Oh, no! She trips! Disaster! Calamity!
"It's all over!" I think.

But somebody doesn't think it is over.
No, somebody thinks it is just
beginning. Somebody with
big black eyes, somebody
with pointy ears, somebody . . .

... wearing my tutu!

The audience gasps.
"It's a dog!" someone shouts.
"Dogs don't do ballet!"

My dog turns bright red and looks at his feet.
"That's what I've always said," Dad mutters.
But then the orchestra starts to play . . .

. . . and my dog dances like no dog
has ever danced before.
Plié! Jeté! Arabesque! Pirouette!

He is as light as a sugarpuff!
As pretty as a fairy!
The audience can't believe it.
"Hooray!" I shout. "That's my dog!"

When the music stops, my dog
gives a hopeful curtsey and blinks
nervously into the spotlight. The theatre is
so very quiet that you could hear a bubble pop.

Then the lady in the front row stands up.
"It's a dog!" she shouts.
Biff's ears start to droop again.

"A dog that does ballet!" she adds. "Bravo!"
Suddenly the whole audience cheers and throws
bunches of roses. My dog glows pink with happiness.
"I don't believe it," says Dad, shaking his head.
"Biff IS a ballerina after all!"
"See," I say proudly, ruffling Biff's ears,
"Dogs DO do ballet. Bravo, Biff!"